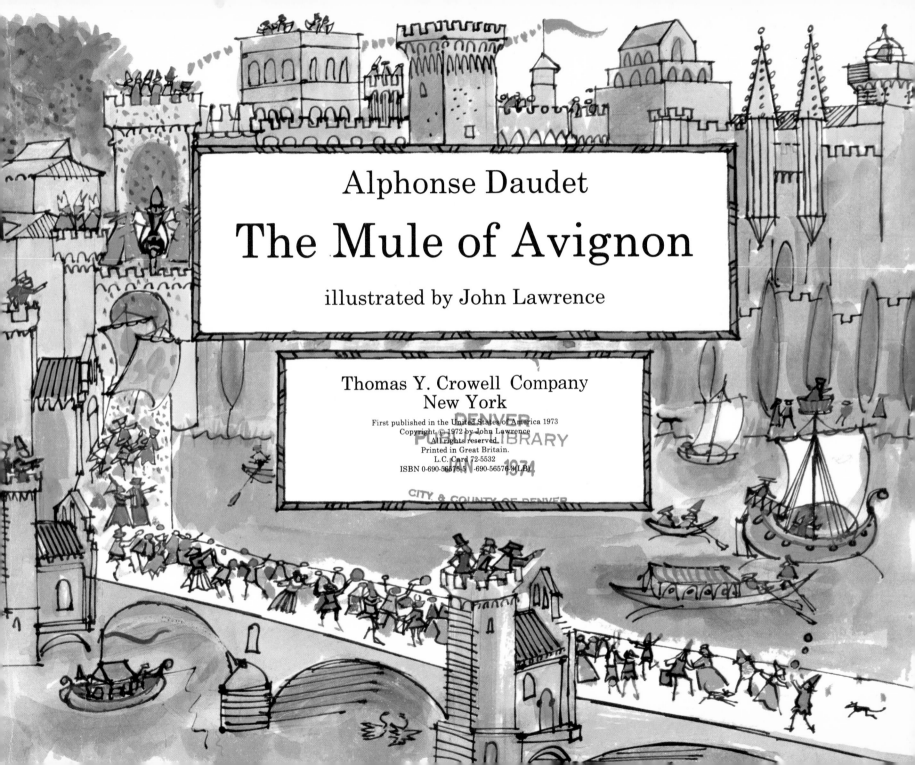

Alphonse Daudet

The Mule of Avignon

illustrated by John Lawrence

Thomas Y. Crowell Company
New York

First published in the United States of America 1973
Copyright © 1972 by John Lawrence
All rights reserved.
Printed in Great Britain.
L.C. Card 72-5532
ISBN 0-690-56575-5 -690-56576-3(LB)

A long time ago the Popes did not live in Rome,
as the Pope does today. They lived in a great palace
at Avignon, in France. The streets of the town
between the busy houses of lacemakers, goldsmiths,
lutemakers and weavers were decorated with flowers
and tapestries and filled with happy people.

In Avignon, when people were happy, they wanted to dance, and the best place for dancing was the bridge over the river Rhône. There they danced to the music of fifes and drums and watched the boats coming up the river with banners streaming in the wind.

The people of Avignon were prosperous and peaceful. They had no king, but were ruled kindly and wisely by the Popes. There was one Pope called Boniface who was loved even more than the others had been. As he rode through the town on his mule, he would smile at everyone, rich or poor, and bless them.

Boniface had two things that he loved most of all.
The first was the little vineyard he had planted himself.
On Sunday afternoons he would sit there in the sunshine
with the cardinals, who were his advisors, his mule by his
side, and pour himself some wine made from his own grapes.

When night began to fall, Boniface would cross the bridge on his way home. As they passed the drummers his mule would dance a step or two and Boniface would nod in time to the music. And all the people would say, "What a good kind Pope he is!"

The second thing Pope Boniface loved was his mule. Every evening before going to bed, he went to her stable to see that she had all she needed, and he always took her a large bowl of red wine mixed with sugar and spice, carrying it himself, in spite of his cardinals' frowns.

The mule was beautiful, with a large, broad back for the Pope to sit on, and she was as gentle and sweet-tempered as an angel. Everyone in Avignon loved her, and treated her kindly—and besides, they knew that for anyone to be kind to the Pope's mule was the best way to fame and fortune.

Tistet Vedene, the goldsmith's son, knew it too. His father had turned him out of the house because he was so lazy.

Since then he had done no work, but he had made a plan —a plan about the Pope's mule.

One day he managed to meet Pope Boniface
alone with his mule. "What a beautiful
animal!" he exclaimed admiringly. "Nobody
else in the world has such a fine mule as yours,
Holy Father!" He stroked the mule and called
her his precious jewel, his pearl...

Boniface was pleased and said to himself, "What a nice little boy!"
And the very next day Tistet Vedene was invited to live in the Pope's
household. He was given a violet silk cloak to wear instead of his
dusty old jacket. His plan had worked.

Now he was in the Pope's service, Tistet laid more plans. He pretended to love the Pope's mule and to care only for her comfort. He made sure he was seen bringing oats or hay or grapes to the stable. Soon the Pope put Tistet in charge of the stable and even allowed him to take the mule her bowl of wine after supper.

Each evening, through the stable door there came a warm, spicy, sugary smell, followed by Tistet Vedene carrying the bowl of wine. But behind him were five or six little boys who burst into the mule's stable and rolled about in her straw. And then the teasing began...

They pulled her ears and tail, climbed on her back, poked her sides
and even drank her bowl of wine.

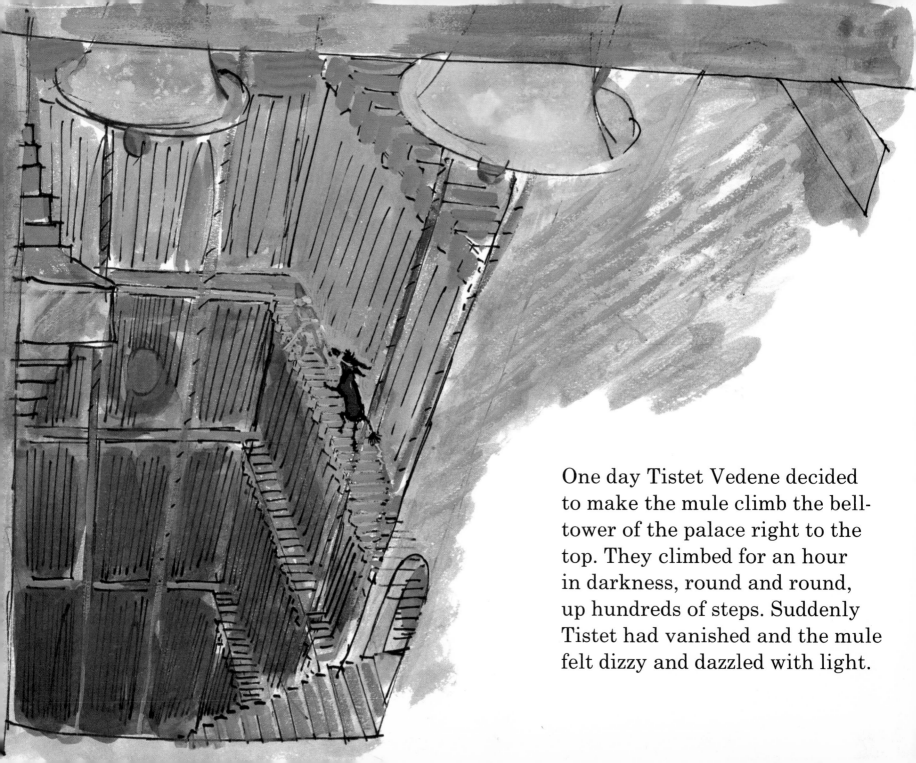

One day Tistet Vedene decided
to make the mule climb the bell-
tower of the palace right to the
top. They climbed for an hour
in darkness, round and round,
up hundreds of steps. Suddenly
Tistet had vanished and the mule
felt dizzy and dazzled with light.

There she was, standing alone
on the platform at the top.
She was terrified.

Far below she could see all Avignon. The stalls in the market-place looked as small as hazel-nuts, the soldiers outside the barracks the size of little red ants, and the river like a silver thread, with tiny people dancing on the bridge across it.

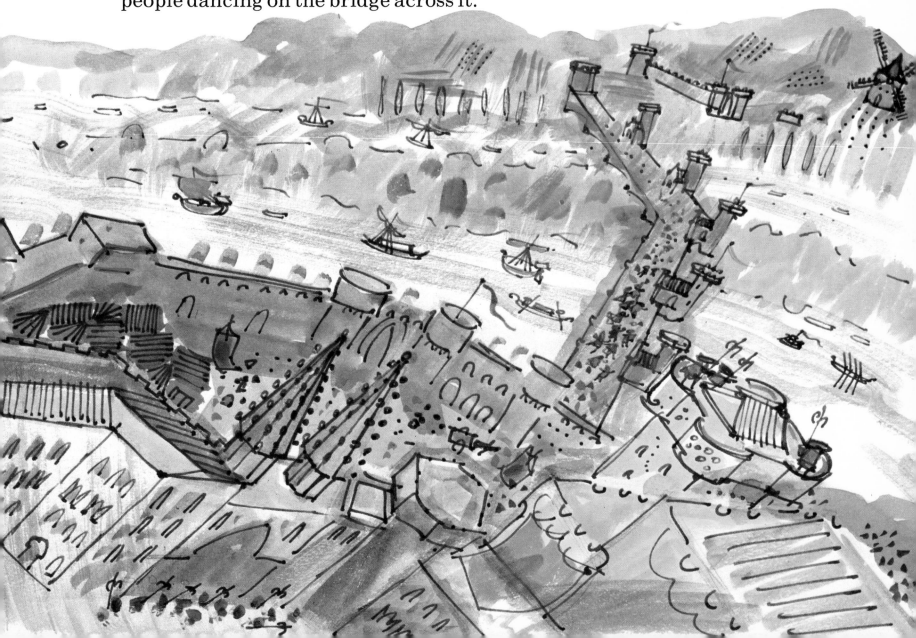

What a fright she had! She gave a shriek which shook all the windows of the palace. The Pope rushed out on to his balcony. Tistet Vedene was already in the courtyard pretending to cry.

"Holy Father, look! Your mule has climbed the bell-tower all by herself. You can just see the tips of her ears waving about up there."

"She'll kill herself!" said the Pope. "She must have gone mad. Come down, you silly animal!"

But how? It was bad going up, but getting down…She would break her legs.

Tistet Vedene was busy telling everyone about his plans to rescue her.

At last the Pope's servants
managed to get her down.
One of the cardinals covered
her eyes with his handkerchief.
Then she had to be lowered in slings
with ropes and pulleys in the most
undignified way. How ashamed
she felt to be hanging in the air
at that great height, her hoofs
waving about, and everyone
in the town watching her disgrace!
At least she was on the side of the
tower where the Pope couldn't see her.

That night the poor mule
couldn't sleep. If she closed
her eyes she seemed to be
back on that horrible platform.
Then suddenly she thought of
what she could do to get even
with Tistet Vedene next morning.
She would give him a kick
to remember. What a kick that
would be! They would see
the smoke of it as far
away as Pamperigouste.

But next morning Tistet Vedene did not come to see the mule. Instead he went down the river to a better job in the Pope's service at Naples. Boniface had rewarded him for his part in rescuing the mule from the tower.

The mule was furious when she heard he had escaped her. Go off to Naples, she thought, but when you come back, I'll have something waiting for you!

Seven years passed before Tistet Vedene came back to Avignon.

Quiet happy days returned for the mule.
No more nasty boys in her stable, but delicious
bowls of spiced wine, snoozes in the sun at the
vineyard, little dances on the bridge over the Rhône.
But nobody, not even the Pope, seemed to trust
her as they once did. They nudged each other
and grinned as she went by, and the Pope
sometimes wondered if on one of his rides
he might not wake up at the top of the tower.

But at last Tistet Vedene came back from Naples. He wanted an even better job. He hoped to become Chief Mustard Maker, which was a high and important position in Avignon.

Tistet had grown tall and good-looking.
He went to see the Pope at once.
"Holy Father," he said, "do you still
have your mule? Is she well? I missed her
so much while I was in Naples. May I see
her again? I've come to see you now on
a very small matter—to ask for the post
of Chief Mustard Maker."

The Pope was touched that Tistet
remembered his mule and said,
"Come tomorrow, and I shall appoint you
Chief Mustard Maker in the presence
of my cardinals. Then you'll see my mule
and you shan't be parted from her ever
again. After that we'll go to my vineyard."

Tistet Vedene was very happy and
waited impatiently for the next day.
But someone in the palace was even
happier and more impatient than he was.
The mule had been stuffing herself with
oats, building up her strength, and
stretching out her back legs,
practising for her part next day.

At last Tistet Vedene came into the courtyard of the palace. He was handsome with his blond curly hair and pointed beard and richly dressed in a scarlet jacket and a hat with a great plume of feathers.

All the cardinals were there, and every single other person of importance. Tistet Vedene bowed low and moved towards the place where the Pope was waiting. At the foot of the steps the mule stood ready to carry the Pope to his vineyard.

Tistet Vedene, making sure the Pope was watching, stopped to give the mule a friendly pat. The mule took a deep breath—

Take THAT! she almost seemed to say, *I've been keeping this carefully, specially for you, for seven whole years!*

And she gave him such a kick that even in distant Pamperigouste they could see the cloud of white smoke rising like a whirlwind, with the plume of white feathers floating above it.

That was all that was ever seen of Tistet Vedene.

Mules don't kick like that any more. But that was a special kick, by a Pope's mule, who, after all, had been waiting seven long years for that wonderful moment.